D0603728

To Jerry, Don, Fred, and Norman,
The Camp Club Men's Auxiliary —E.S.

For Victor, who guided my hand and my vision —R.C.

☆ ☆ ☆ ☆

Published by Dial Books for Young Readers
A division of Penguin Putnam Inc.
345 Hudson Street
New York, New York 10014

Text copyright © 2003 by Eileen Spinelli
Pictures copyright © 2003 by Raúl Colón
All rights reserved
Designed by Nancy R. Leo-Kelly
Text set in Opti-Packard
Manufactured in China on acid-free paper
1 3 5 7 9 10 8 6 4 2

Library of Congress Cataloging-in-Publication Data
Spinelli, Eileen.
Rise the moon / Eileen Spinelli; pictures by Raúl Colón.
p.   cm.
Summary: A variety of people and animals are touched by an enchanting moonlit night.
ISBN 0-8037-2601-5
[1. Moon—Fiction. 2. Stories in rhyme.] I. Colón, Raúl, ill. II. Title.
PZ8.3.S759 Ri 2003   [E]—dc21   00-034623

The full-color artwork was prepared using watercolors.
The paintings were then scratched, scraped, and etched before colored pencils were applied.

RISE

THE

MOON

Eileen Spinelli ☆ pictures by *Raúl Colón*

Dial Books for Young Readers *New York*

Rise the moon
and lunar moth,
drawn to its lovely shine,
flits across the blossoms
of the dreamy moonflower vine.

While in a rooftop attic
in the quiet hush of night,
a moonlit artist
takes his brush
to paint a bowl of light.

A downstairs dancer
climbs up to
the dappled roof alone
to do a graceful moon-dance
on her neighbor's garden stone.

A night-shift baker
rolls a moon-shaped crust
for apple pie
as moony tomcat
yowls atop
an alley fence nearby.

And, oh, the sleepy sailor
on the swaying schooner knows
it is the pull of moon
by which the ocean
comes and goes.

Sea turtles launch themselves
across a breezy dune
toward the surf
that's speckled golden
by the midnight moon.

The silver wolf
is called to howl
its ancient moonstruck song.
Others in the pack join in:
a haunting sing-along.

The cozy camper
reads by moonlight
and a tired hiker sees
a welcome path of moonbeams
through the darkened trees.

Astronomers
star-party
on the soaring mountain slopes
to watch the distant moon-face
through skyward telescopes.

Moon-wakened mouse
goes gathering,
so busy and so brave,
while bat awakens
upside down
and flutters from her cave.

Some farmers
follow faithfully
this old advice indeed:
that moonrise
is the wisest time
for planting pumpkin seed.

Young mother
swings by moon-glow
beneath the leafy boughs,
while baby dreams
of Mother Goose
and moons and jumping cows.

So rise the moon,
so round and bright,
let its tender magic fall.
Within its spell of splendor
we are
moon-hearted creatures
all.